AMONG THE DOLLS

This can't be happening, Vicky said to herself. It's impossible! I must be dreaming. But it wasn't vague like a dream. Everything was horribly clear, and all the details were perfect. She tried to fight a growing panic, which was only made worse by the deep void just ahead of her.

Behind her, the music stopped with a sudden crash and she spun around. Beside the music box stood the aunt doll, taller than Vicky now. In the abrupt silence, Vicky simply stared at her without speaking.

"Aha," said the aunt doll softly, her smiling mouth not moving at all. "You are small and helpless now, I see."

Among the Dolls

WILLIAM SLEATOR

SCHOLASTIC INC.
New York   Toronto   London   Auckland   Sydney
Mexico City   New Delhi   Hong Kong   Buenos Aires

ISBN-13: 978-0-545-00017-8
ISBN-10: 0-545-00017-3

Copyright © 1975 by William Sleator.
Reader's Guide © 2006 by Tor Books.
All rights reserved. Published by Scholastic Inc., 557 Broadway, New York, NY 10012, by arrangement with St. Martin's Press, LLC. SCHOLASTIC and associated logos are trademarks and/or registered trademarks of Scholastic Inc.

12 11 10 9 8 7 6 5 4 3 2 1   7 8 9 10 11 12/0

Printed in the U.S.A.   40

First Scholastic printing, February 2007

Chapter One

The poplar trees along the roadside shimmered in a light breeze, and there was hardly a nip in the autumn air. It was altogether a perfect day for a family outing. Certainly it did not occur to Vicky to wonder about what the approaching, more bitter season would hold for her.

What she was thinking about more than anything else as they drove along the winding country road was the ten-speed bicycle she hoped to get for her birthday.

Her father looked briefly back at her from the driver's seat and smiled. "You haven't said a word for miles, Vicky," he said. "Something on your mind?"

"Oh," she said dreamily, trying not to make the hint too obvious, "I was just thinking about what a wonderful place this would be to go for rides on a brand new, ten—"

"Wait! Stop!" her mother cried out, startling Vicky and not giving her a chance to finish. Her father pulled the car abruptly over to the side of the road where there was a hand-lettered ANTIQUES sign nailed to a tree. Vicky sighed. Her mother was always searching for old phonograph records and sheet music.

Her father winked at Vicky. "It won't take long," he said, and they followed her mother up to the dilapidated wooden farmhouse that sagged behind the sign.

It was dark inside, and there was a moldy basement smell. The room was so crowded with old dusty things that there were only a few narrow corridors for walking. While her mother rummaged through tattered piles, Vicky drifted circuitously through the dimness, trying to decide whether she wanted a yellow bike or a blue one, with racing handlebars, of course, but should the tape be—

Suddenly, from the other side of the room, her father exclaimed over something. Her mother hurried over to him, and they exchanged a few excited whispers. The old woman who had let them in, who was so fat that her legs bent outward and she had to hobble with a cane, seemed particularly pleased about whatever it was they had noticed. Her toothless mouth puckered into a smile; she stood up a little straighter and brushed the hair out of her eyes.

To Vicky's relief they left the farmhouse soon after that, taking nothing with them. As they drove away Vicky caught one last glimpse of the old woman staring at them from the shadowy doorway, her wrinkled face eager with curiosity. Vicky forgot her immediately, however.

"It really is beautiful here," she said dreamily. "The perfect place to go for long rides on a brand new, ten-speed bike."

But her parents, who were now preoccupied in an odd way, did not seem to hear her.

As her birthday approached, her parents grew more and more excited. Vicky was sure they had gotten her the bicycle. And when finally the day arrived and they told her the present was too big to wrap and had been hidden in the basement, she was certain. Hardly daring to look, she kept her eyes closed, hopping with anticipation, as they led her down the stairs.

When she opened her eyes and saw, not the gleaming, streamlined vision she had been imagining, but a musty antique dollhouse with old-fashioned, faded furniture and dolls, her disappointment was too great to hide. Her parents beamed proudly, waiting for her to respond. All she could do was mumble something and look down at her feet.

Vicky cried easily, and the tears started just after her father had carried the dollhouse up to her room. There it sat on the floor across from her bed. It was nearly as tall as she was, and its dark gray Mansard roof and shadowy little rooms cast an aura of gloom over her bright bedroom. All at once she realized that she would have to be alone with it at night. It was the thought of that thing watching and waiting in the darkness, even more than her disappointment about the bicycle, that suddenly brought on her tears.

She struggled to get down her ice cream and cake while her parents asked her over and over again what was wrong. At first they seemed bewildered, then disappointed, as though it were somehow Vicky's fault that the day had gone badly. All of Vicky's explanations seemed childish and silly, and at last they stopped asking. Her mother took away her half-empty plate briskly, without a word. It was undoubtedly the worst birthday she had ever had.

The dollhouse was the first thing she saw when she woke up the day after her birthday, and she turned her head quickly away from it. But, though she tried at first, the dollhouse was impossible to ignore. Not only was it so large, but now she began to be aware that it held a peculiar fascination for her.

She looked more closely at the dolls that belonged in it. With a strange reluctance, she picked them up one by one and turned them over in her hands. There were four of them: a mother, a father, another woman, who she decided must be the aunt, and a little girl. They were all old, and somehow seemed to share the atmosphere of the house, as though they had lived in it for years and years.

And that was what gave her the idea that what the dollhouse needed was one more doll. If there could be something new in it, something that she chose herself, then perhaps the atmosphere would change just a little. She might even dislike the house less.

At first, her mother objected. It was always a mistake to interrupt her when she was playing the old upright piano in the kitchen, but Vicky was too hopeful of her new idea to wait.

"But it won't fit in with the other dolls," her mother explained, sighing, her hands still resting on the keys. "Everything in that house is an antique, it all belongs together. Something new would destroy the atmosphere."

But that, of course, was just what Vicky wanted;

and at last her mother relented. She gave her some money, and Vicky dashed out of the house to the strains of an impatient Chopin Waltz.

Most of the miniature dolls in the department store resembled tall and thin young women, like fashion models. Vicky lingered over them for awhile, but at last decided against any of them. Not only did they seem to be too large, but there was also something in their blank and cold expressions that reminded her of the dolls already in the doll-house. At last she came upon a small plastic toddler with a head too large for his body, a pathetic little face, and short, fat arms and legs. He seemed to be just the right size, and, more important, radiated in-nocence and a gleaming newness.

When she first set him down with the other dolls in the conservatory he stood out uncomfortably, pink and shiny among the gray, dusty figures. But somehow his presence was just what she needed to overcome her repugnance. She began to give in to the pull of the dollhouse.

And it was actually rather amusing to play with the dolls. The mother and the aunt would cook and clean; the father would read and work at his desk; the children played with their toys. They gathered around the dining room table at mealtimes, and re-tired to their beds at night. It was all very calm and pleasant; until one night at dinner the doll family began to fight.

At first there were nothing but uncomfortable little squabbles. The brother would refuse to eat and the mother would send him to his room. The sister would grab one of his toys and claim it was hers. The mother would criticize the father; the aunt would complain that she was working too hard. Gradually, the quarrelsome life in the dollhouse became more dramatic, and day by day more fascinating to Vicky—especially as her own life began to change.

School was a trial for Vicky. She was shy, and never seemed to make any friends. Home had always been the place where she could find peace and comfort. But now that was no longer true.

One day her mother fell down the stairs, breaking her hand, and she was different after that. She couldn't play the piano, and in her frustration began bullying Vicky's father, who strangely enough seemed to be unable to stand up for himself. Nor would he stand up for Vicky anymore, but instead would retire to his basement study when her mother began to scold. And now she scolded and nagged more than she ever had before, criticizing Vicky about her poor grades in school, about the fact that she had no friends. It was so bad that Vicky hardly dared to approach her. Mealtimes were agony.

As her own life became worse, the dolls' arguments grew more intense. The mother doll began to strike the children, to throw things at them, and the daughter would scream insults back at her. The aunt would brutally scrub the children's faces and hands and lock them in their room without supper. The mother would then berate the father, who would fling himself upon his bed and sob.

And then the day came when Vicky brought home her report card, the worst report card she had ever received. When her mother saw what was on it, she flew into a rage and slapped Vicky across the face. She had never struck her before.

The dollhouse that day was blurred through Vicky's tears. Almost too miserable to play, she moved the dolls about dispiritedly, sending the daughter up to her room for throwing food, then creating a long argument between the mother and father over the lunch table, which ended in his retreating to his bed. She had just been about to take the daughter out of her room, when the sunlight coming in through the window had dimmed. Vicky looked up, then felt suddenly dizzy and closed her eyes.

When she opened them she was inside the dollhouse.

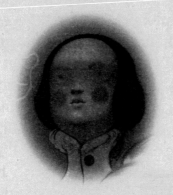

Chapter Two

Vicky blinked and stood up. She knew immediately that she was in the third-floor playroom. There was the tin rocking horse she always made the brother doll ride for hours. Its back looked very sharp and uncomfortable now that she could see it better. There were the "books" she had made for them, from little folded pieces of paper; but now they were like cardboard, covered with large grainy crayon blots.

And there was the music box, barely the size of her thumb the last time she had opened it, but now like a massive chest. It was made of ivory, and the carving, which had seemed so delicate, was actually rather crude and uneven. The little tinkling melody it played over and over again was her favorite song, and suddenly she wanted to hear it. She was frightened, of course, and the familiarity of the unchanging tune might comfort her. She pushed open the box, and the music began.

But it was different now, clanging and blurred and painfully loud, like being on the inside of a ringing bell. And the tune was hardly recognizable, a raucous mockery of its former sweetness. She had to stop it! But the top was caught somehow; she couldn't move it at all. Her hands on her ears, she backed away, then turned to run from the terrible sounds.

But she froze before taking even one step. Now she was facing the edge of the house, where the room simply ended and there was nothing but empty space plunging all the way down to the floor of her room. It was like being in a house that had been neatly sliced down the middle by a gigantic cleaver. She didn't dare get any closer to the edge, but stood and stared off into her room, the horrible music banging and bonging behind her.

Everything was the same, but gigantic. The rug was a thick forest spread out far below her, her bed a steep plateau, and the doorway on the other side of the room was fuzzy with distance, rising up to a ceiling she could not even see.

This can't be happening, she said to herself. It's impossible! I must be dreaming. But it wasn't vague like a dream. Everything was horribly clear, and all the details were perfect. She tried to fight a growing panic, which was only made worse by the deep void just ahead of her. This can't be happening, she thought again, uselessly. I've got to make it go away! How can I make it go away?

Behind her, the music stopped with a sudden crash and she spun around. Beside the music box stood the aunt doll, taller than Vicky now. In the abrupt silence, Vicky simply stared at her without speaking. The doll's black hair, pulled back tightly in a knot at the back of her head, was now like thick rope. The stitches on her floor-length black dress were wide and uneven. Her painted features were chipped in places, giving her smile a strange twisted look. Her lashless eyes were amazingly large, almost circles, opened wide, a black pupil isolated in the center of each.

"Aha," said the aunt doll softly, her smiling mouth not moving at all. "You are small and helpless now, I see."

Chapter Three

"Wh-what?" Vicky said. "What do you mean?" She could not take her eyes from the doll's face. It seemed impossible that a voice could come from that painted mask. But it did come, quiet and dark and cold.

"You shall see," she said. "Come with me to the dining room."

Vicky followed her through the doorway to the stairway in the center of the house. She had never noticed how steep it was; it was very dark, and the going was difficult. She hardly dared to think what would happen if she should slip and bump against the aunt, who was bobbing stiffly down just ahead of her.

From the third floor they descended past the living room and the conservatory, with its potted palms, on the second. Down another flight of stairs they came to the dining room, which shared the first floor with the kitchen.

She expected to see all the dolls sitting around the table. Then she remembered that she had put the father in his bedroom (he was probably still lying on the bed and crying), and shut the daughter up in hers. The aunt stepped through the dining room doorway ahead of her, then turned back, and with her hard wooden hand on Vicky's neck, pushed her into the room. "Look who we have here," she said.

The mother sat at one end of the long table. Her hair was in its usual disarray, the pinkish-blonde curls floating stiffly around her cherubic face with its little red dot of a mouth, round cheeks, and innocent blue eyes. Beside her sat the brother, staring down at his plate.

"Well!" said the mother doll, and hid her face for a moment, giggling. A few strands of her quivering hair fell down onto her plate. "Well!" she repeated, looking up again. "Don't just stand there staring at me like an imbecile! Sit down, sit down!" Her voice was piercing and quick, like a record played too fast. "Dandaroo! Arrange a chair for our *guest.*"

Silently, still not looking up, the brother rose and pulled out the chair beside him. The painted features on his flat plastic face were already beginning to fade from the repeated rough washings administered by the aunt, giving him a curiously noseless appearance. His head was as large as his torso, and his short, plump legs had no knees. Uncomfortably, Vicky sat down. The mother's behavior was disturbing; and her strident, harsh manner was made all the more eerie by her unchanging expression of angelic idiocy.

"You sit down too, Diadama," she squealed at the aunt. "We have lots and *lots* to talk about. You know we do.

"Now," said the mother, turning back to Vicky, "I would offer you something to eat but of course there isn't anything, except that revolting plaster turkey that's been sitting in the middle of the table for years. You may have some of that if you'd like."

"Er, no thank you," Vicky said timidly.

"No, of course there isn't anything to eat," the mother went on as if she hadn't heard her, "because you know as well as I do that dolls can't eat. Yet day after day here we sit in front of these empty plates, staring at that beastly turkey and bickering with each other, endlessly bickering. And why? I'll tell you why, my dear little girl. Because *you* make us!"

"I—" said Vicky.

"Do not interrupt, child," said the aunt in her cold voice. "Remember, you are small and helpless now."

"But—" said Vicky.

"Not to mention all the other things you make us do," the mother continued. "The way we have to lie in those beds for endless hours every night. The way we have to stand in that meaningless kitchen, cooking with empty pots. And the way you make us fight all the time, and lock each other in our rooms. Not that I haven't begun to enjoy—" Suddenly she looked toward the door. "Why, Quimbee," she said. "Tired of sulking? Then come in and sit down. Look who's here."

Naturally she wouldn't have heard the father doll coming downstairs, Vicky realized as he sat down meekly beside the mother. Unlike the aunt and the mother, who were wooden, or the plastic son, the father doll was soft. His arms and legs were nothing but pipe cleaners; his head and body simply wads of cotton with cloth wrapped tightly around them. His face was stitched with thread—the prim pink line of his mouth, the thin black mustache, the vacant brown knots that were his eyes. He wore a black suit, and nothing protruded from the ends of his tubular sleeves and trousers, for they had been made just long enough to conceal the fact that he had no hands or feet.

"Now!" said the mother. "If only Ganglia would come down out of her room we'd all be here for this momentous occasion."

"G-Ganglia?" said Vicky, horrified. "That isn't the sister's name, is it? It couldn't be!"

"And why not!" snapped the mother. "You never bothered to give us names. We had to do it ourselves. And Ganglia," she went on, snickering, "suits her personality perfectly."

"It does *not*!" shrieked a voice from the doorway. "Not one bit! *Your* name should be Ganglia."

"Do not speak that way to your mother," said the aunt.

"You can't tell me what to do, you old goat. I'll talk any way I want," said the sister doll as she flounced into the room. Flouncing came easily to her, for she was made of rubber and could move her arms and legs in any direction. Vicky had spent hours putting her through grotesque contortions, leaving her tied up in knots for days at a time, lying helplessly in the middle of the dining room table while the others stared at her placidly over empty teacups.

"Look who's here," said the mother.

"I know," Ganglia said, plopping down at the table. She turned to look at Vicky, her one eye glittering. (The other had fallen out weeks ago.) Over the years, the cracks covering her face had filled with black grime; and now they twisted into a kind of smile. "Yes, I know who she is all right."

"She is powerless now," said the aunt.

"Exactly," the mother said. "Very well put, Diadama."

They were all staring at her except the brother, who was still looking at his plate. "But I don't understand," said Vicky, growing more and more uneasy as she looked from one malevolent gaze to another. "I didn't think you were like . . . like this. Why are you looking at me so strangely?"

"You *should* understand," said the aunt. "It is you, after all, who has made us what we are."

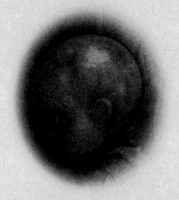

Chapter Four

Vicky was running up the stairs. Behind her she could hear the shouting and confusion caused by her sudden departure from the dining room. Fortunately, none of the dolls could move as quickly as she, for they were all quite stiff except for Ganglia, who kept tripping over her own feet.

Made them what they are? Vicky wondered as she hurried through the shadows, barking her shins continually on the steep steps. What did that mean?

She was panting by the time she dashed into the playroom. She had entered the dollhouse through this room, and without thinking about it she had assumed that it might be the way to escape. But how? she wondered frantically. It was far too high to jump; and there was no way to climb down. She could hear the dolls on the stairs below her, arguing in high-pitched voices. And then the gigantic door in the distance swung open, and her mother stepped into the room.

"Mother!" Vicky screamed, "Mother, help me! I'm here, in the dollhouse."

"Vicky?" her mother said crossly, looking around the room, and for a moment Vicky thought she had heard her. But her mother's eyes swept past the dollhouse as if it weren't there.

"Mother!" she screamed again. "Here! Over here! Oh, help me! In the dollhouse, I'm in the *doll*house!"

Casually, her mother bent down to pick up a shoe lying in the middle of the floor. She tossed it in the direction of the closet, then moved toward the dollhouse.

"Mother, I'm here!" Vicky kept screaming, jumping up and down and waving her arms. She could hear the dolls getting closer, Ganglia's squeals rising above the other voices. But her mother, staring abstractedly down at the house from her great height, noticed nothing. In a moment, she walked briskly out of the room.

Vicky dropped her arms to her sides, tears streaming down her cheeks. The dolls were just outside the door now. There was nowhere to go, so she simply sank to her knees in the middle of the floor, helpless, as the dolls clattered into the room. They seemed relieved to see her there.

"Look!" Ganglia shrieked, her arms flailing as she staggered to a stop. "She's crying!"

"Why, so she is," said the father, with a nervous titter. His voice was muffled and thick, as though his mouth were full of cotton, which it was.

"Well . . ." said the mother, nodding. They stood in a group, watching her.

Vicky wiped her eyes. "I . . . I want to get out," she said. "And my mother came into the room, but . . . but she couldn't even see me, or hear me." Her eyes filled with tears again.

"No, of course she couldn't," said the mother doll. "You're in *our* world now. You probably just looked like another doll to her."

"And it is no use trying to get out," said the aunt. "It is no use. There is a barrier."

"Barrier?" said Vicky. "What do you mean?"

"Oh, when you were out there you could take us in and out, of course," said the mother. "But no one inside the house can get out on his own."

"You mean I have to stay here forever?" Vicky gasped.

"Does she?" said Ganglia.

Suddenly the dolls were clustered together, muttering secretively to one another. "How long . . . Did it ever . . . Your fault . . . No! No! I tell you it . . . Have to . . . only thing . . . But why . . . Yes! I insist . . . Will she . . . Small and helpless . . . Big surprise. . . ."

At last they stepped apart. "I don't have to stay here forever, do I?" Vicky asked again, terrified.

"Perhaps you do and perhaps you don't," said the mother, with a toss of her head that sent several pink hairs fluttering to the floor.

"But . . . ," said Vicky, beginning to cry again, "But. . . ."

"Oh, stop it!" said Ganglia, stamping her foot so hard that her leg bent double and she almost tipped over. Righting herself, she put her hands on her hips and glared at Vicky. "It won't do you any good to keep blubbering like that. It's getting sickening. You'll find out sooner or later. And what's wrong with being here, anyway?" She stretched out her neck toward Vicky.

"Quimbee. Dandaroo," the mother said, turning to the father and brother and nodding at them meaningfully. "Remember what we decided. It's time now."

"Hmmm, yes, yes I suppose it is," mumbled the father. "Come, Dandaroo." The brother followed him reluctantly out of the room.

"Time for what?" Vicky asked, wondering if it had anything to do with her.

"It's not time for anything," snapped the mother.

"None of your business," Ganglia said quickly.

"One does not ask one's hostess such questions," said the aunt.

"Oh, I'm sorry," Vicky said, now even more curious, but afraid to ask them anything else.

"Well, don't you want to see the rest of the house?" Ganglia said suddenly.

"I . . . I guess so."

"Well, come on, then."

She followed Ganglia out of the room, to the stairway. And there, at the very top of the stairs, was a narrow doorway that, since the landing was very small and dark, she had never noticed before.

Though still rather numb with fear and confusion, Vicky was nevertheless surprised. "Hey," she said, stopping. "I never knew that doorway was there. Where does it go?"

The aunt and the mother were rustling behind her. "It goes nowhere," said the mother, suddenly pushing her across the landing to the room beyond. "It's just an artifice. There's nothing behind it. Ganglia, show her the bedrooms. We have to go talk to Quimbee and Dandaroo, *downstairs*." She said this last word with great significance, and then started downstairs with the aunt, as Ganglia pulled Vicky into the room.

The bedrooms were across the stairs from the playroom. There were only two of them, and they were small, having been made by dividing a room the size of the playroom in half.

"This is where me and Dandaroo go to bed," Ganglia said, still walking, as though in a hurry to get Vicky into the further bedroom. "As if you didn't know it. Why did you put that oaf in here with me anyway? I wish I had my own room."

"But there were only two bedrooms," Vicky explained, trying to think clearly. "And so one had to be yours and the other one your parents'."

"Well, you could have put one of these beds in the playroom, couldn't you, and made that my room?" Ganglia paused to think. "Then I'd have the biggest bedroom of all, and all the toys too."

"Uh, maybe I'll do that, when I . . . I mean, if I ever do get out. In fact," Vicky went on, growing suddenly hopeful as a brilliant idea occurred to her, "in fact, I promise I will. If you help me get out, I promise I'll make it your room, and put more toys there too."

"Hmmm," Ganglia said, folding her arms across

her chest and letting her one eye rove thoughtfully across the ceiling. "I'll think about it. . . ."

"And if there's anything else you want, I'll do that too," Vicky continued frantically. "Just tell me what it is. If you help me get out, I'll do it, I promise I will."

"I said I'd think about it!" Ganglia shouted, stamping her foot again.

Vicky shrank away from her. "Okay," she stammered. "I'm sorry."

"Well, you should be! And come on in here," Ganglia went on impatiently. "Don't you want to see their room too?"

The bed in the parents' room was made of wood with tall, carved posts. There wasn't room for much else, and though of course she was interested in seeing all of the house, it did seem strange that Ganglia should seem so eager to get her into this room. There was really nothing to do there, but Ganglia slumped down on the bed as if she wanted to stay for awhile, saying, "Why don't you sit down?"

Vicky sat as far away from Ganglia as possible. The bed was extremely hard and uncomfortable, she noted with surprise; and then remembered that of course it would be, for there was nothing under the blanket but a block of wood.

"Not too comfy, is it?" Ganglia said, seeing the look on Vicky's face.

"No, I guess it isn't."

"And my bed's just the same. I'll bet you never wondered what it felt like to sleep on one of these things, did you?"

"No, I didn't," Vicky admitted. "But . . . do you really sleep?"

"No, but we have to lie here for hours, because you make us."

"I'm sorry," Vicky said. "I know I've done a lot of things you didn't like. But how could I know you were alive, that you felt things, that you cared what I did to you? If I'd known, I'm sure I wouldn't have treated you the same way."

"Hmph!" Ganglia snorted. "*I'm* not so sure."

At that moment there was a faint noise from the stairway, as though a door were being opened very carefully. Vicky stood up. "Who's on the stairs out there?" she said, moving toward the door. "I thought everyone else was downstairs."

"They are! They are!" Ganglia cried, leaping from the bed and running to stand in front of the doorway, so that Vicky could not get out of the room.

"But I heard a noise—"

"What noise? I didn't hear any noise. There was no noise."

But just then Vicky thought she heard the sound of descending footsteps: one pair like heavy feet trying to be quiet, the other only a soft patter. It was difficult to tell if they were really there, however, for suddenly Ganglia was talking incessantly in her loud, high-pitched voice.

"Everyone's downstairs, there's nobody else up here; you were imagining it. Isn't that an ugly picture over the bed? Don't you just hate the wallpaper in here? You're wearing such a pretty dress; I wish I had a dress like that; I always have to wear the same dress all the time; why don't you ever change my clothes?"

And on she babbled, while Vicky stood there, trying, but unable, to hear more. Someone, she was almost sure, had come out of that little doorway at the top of the stairs.

Chapter Five

They all gathered before dinner in the conservatory.

"Getting hungry, Vicky?" said the mother, watching her with the expression of amused surprise that never left her face.

"No, not really."

"That's just as well, because, as you know, there's nothing in the house to eat. Yet here we sit, preparing to go into the dining room and sit *there* for no reason, staring idiotically at each other, all just so we can fit into your little scheme of how—"

"Will you get *off*!" cried Ganglia. "It's my seat, I tell you!" She and Dandaroo were fighting over the little ottoman. He had been there first, but now she was sitting on the edge, trying to push him off. Stolidly, looking at the floor, he refused to move, while she kept banging herself against him until her arm was bent all out of shape.

"But I'm not making you do anything now," Vicky said to the mother, raising her voice in order to be heard over Ganglia's grunts and squeals.

"Yes, but one falls into patterns," said the mother doll, with a little sigh of resignation. "Even if you didn't come near us for a month, we'd still be doing this."

"We would still be what you have made us," the aunt said darkly.

"Yes, we would still be what you have made us," agreed the mother, nodding, and several glinting hairs drifted down to the oriental rug. Everywhere she went she left little piles of her hair behind her; Vicky had never before noticed how thin it was on the top of her head. "Not," the mother went on, "that I really *mind* being this way. I rather enjoy this streak of cruelty you've—Ganglia!" she shrieked suddenly, spinning around in her chair and knocking Ganglia to the floor with one quick swipe of her fat arm. "Will you shut up!"

"But he's on my chair," Ganglia wailed, writhing snakelike against the red and blue pattern on the rug.

"Well . . . ," said the mother thoughtfully, "yes, I suppose he is." Her voice became firm. "Dandaroo, get off her chair this instant."

"But," said Dandaroo in a thin, reedlike voice, "I

was here first, and she never decided whose chair was whose in this room." He looked at Vicky.

"If Ganglia says it's hers, it is hers," declared the mother. She pointed at the door. "To your room."

But as he left, still looking, strangely enough, right at her, Vicky almost thought she saw a flicker of expression cross his fading features. It was an expression of resentment, but mingled with pity. But who was he pitying? Could it be her?

What you have made us. The aunt's words lingered in her mind as she followed the dolls downstairs to the dining room. She was beginning to understand. The rough and violent things she had made them do had become their personalities. She had created them, and now they were turned against her. She shivered on the dark stairway. What were they going to do to her? So far they hadn't really done anything, but she could feel a crackle of anticipation in the air, as though some secret plan against her were evolving.

She stopped walking and, trembling slightly, stood on the stairs and considered running away from them again. But now she knew it would do no good. The only solution was to get out of the house, if only there were some way to do it. She felt tears springing to her eyes at the thought of being caught here forever, but she quickly brushed them away, took a deep breath, and started after the dolls again.

It was the thought of the doorway at the top of the stairs that kept her from giving way to despair. The mother had said it wasn't real, but she was almost sure she had heard it open and footsteps coming from it. When Ganglia had finally let her out of the bedroom, she had looked all over the house and found no one new who could have come out of the door.

So perhaps that was where Quimbee and Dandaroo had gone, and it was their footsteps she had heard. Somehow, she felt that something very important was beyond that door, and she was determined now to get through it. But she had to wait for the right moment. If she tried now, they would stop her, and she dreaded to think what they would do to her then.

The dining room was on the first floor. Just beyond it she could see her bedroom carpet, stretching hazily off into the distance in the fading afternoon light. Each thick strand was as high as her knee.

"So near and yet so far, eh Vicky?" said the mother, noticing her wistful glance. "You could always try just stepping out there, I suppose, if you wanted to spend the rest of your life the size of a doll. It sounds rather amusing at first thought, doesn't it? But you'd probably get quite tired of things like climbing those huge stairs and fending off cats, and come crawling back to us in the end, I expect."

"There is a barrier," said the aunt.

"Oh, yes, there is a barrier," the mother agreed, sitting down languidly. "You may try getting through it if you like." Her eyes came to rest on the turkey. "Ugh! How I hate that thing. So revoltingly naked."

Vicky couldn't resist. She was sure they were right about the barrier, but she could not see it, and the thought of getting away from them was unbearably tempting. Feeling their eyes on her, she stepped toward the edge. But at the threshold it became difficult to move forward, as though some great force were pushing against her. She struggled, using every bit of strength she had, but the force was so strong that, even leaning with all her weight against it, she did not move at all. When she turned back to the room, the pressure was suddenly gone.

Ganglia was giggling at her, one hand over her mouth. "Didn't she look funny?" she said. "All panting and puffy. And look at her hair."

Vicky brushed back her hair, which had fallen

into her eyes, and sat miserably down at the table. Ganglia's taunts were hard to bear. Think of the door, she said to herself. Think of the door.

Getting through it might be difficult, however, for at least one of them was always watching her. As she sat at the table she studied each of the dolls' faces in turn, trying to decide which of them, if any, might be persuaded to help her. For there was one other hopeful thing, and that was the power she would have over them when she did get out.

She could put a proposal to them all at once, that she would do anything any of them wanted; but that wouldn't work because she was sure that each would selfishly want whatever she promised to someone else. They would never agree. And remembering her conversation with Ganglia in the bedroom, it seemed that bribing them individually might be more effective. After all, it wouldn't much matter what it was she promised them; to the dolls, whatever she offered would be enticing only if it were something the others couldn't have.

She discarded the aunt at once. She was so distant and cold that Vicky was afraid to say anything to her. She would never have the nerve to ask her for help. The father, who had entered the dining room, was of no use. He was so utterly meek and helpless that he probably wouldn't dare to help her, even if she offered him everything she could think of. And Dandaroo, who was still up in his room, would be the same.

Although. . . .

Her eyes slid back to the father's face. The cotton in his head seemed to be settling down, so that the top of his head was narrow and empty and his chin was wide, sagging down onto his chest. He was staring vacantly at the wall, while on either side of him Ganglia and the mother, both giggling, were stabbing savagely at the turkey with their knives and forks, crumbling off bits of plaster. The father . . . what if she promised him that when she got out she would make him the ruler of the family; that everyone else would follow his orders, that they would treat him like a king and bow and scrape at his every whim? He might not be able to resist that. And he didn't seem as cruel as the others; he might even want to help her, if he knew that he would be safe afterward. He was definitely a possibility.

It was different with the mother. She was already in control. And Ganglia she couldn't trust. She had almost seemed to respond in the bedroom, but Vicky was sure that she would take great joy in exposing her little scheme to all the others. No; it was the father or no one.

But as Vicky watched him, her hopes sank. His

sagging cheeks twitched nervously. Perhaps he might like to have control over them all, but he would be too timid to take any risk. Before asking him, she must try to get out on her own.

Tonight, she decided, when they were all in bed, she would go through the secret door by herself.

Chapter Six

At night, the dollhouse was very dark.

Vicky should have expected it, knowing that the house had no lights. But she had not been prepared for the hush that fell over everything, for the huge, oddly-shaped shadows that crept across her rug like jagged mountain peaks, silently gliding into the house, crawling up the stairs, and filling all the rooms. Around her the dolls' faces slowly vanished into the darkness, until she could not see them at all, but only hear the faint rustle of a skirt, or the creak of a wooden joint.

But even in the darkness, she could feel the alertness of their eyes upon her. They sat without speaking, strangely transfixed, as though waiting for something to happen. And from the way they were watching, Vicky guessed that it was something that was going to happen to her.

At last she could not stand it any longer, and stood up suddenly from the table. The dolls stood up too.

"Going somewhere, Vicky?" came the mother's voice, sounding even more menacing and sarcastic in the darkness. "I think we would like to come with you."

"I just . . . I want to go to bed. I'm tired," Vicky said, thinking of the secret door, and hoping she would be able to get away from them.

"Tired?" said the mother. "You poor little thing. And where were you planning to sleep, may I ask?"

"I—I don't know."

"She doesn't know," said the mother, and Vicky heard the squeak of her neck as she nodded invisibly. (Her head was the only part of her that moved very easily, Vicky remembered; no wonder she nodded all the time.)

Ganglia stifled an excited giggle, and then the aunt spoke. "If you had thought to make things more comfortable for us, then perhaps there would be somewhere for you to sleep now."

Vicky thought of the hard beds and then remembered, feeling a chill, that she had never provided any place at all for the aunt to sleep. She would just leave her sitting stiffly by herself in the dining room, or, and she shuddered at the thought, in some undignified place like under the kitchen table. Certainly, the aunt would never forgive her for that.

They seemed to be waiting for her to make some reply. "Well," she began haltingly, "I just always thought that, you know, that it didn't really matter to you, that you couldn't tell the difference, since you were only dolls and—"

There was a sharp gasp all around her, and she stopped, putting her hand quickly over her mouth. "Oh, I'm sorry," she went on, "I didn't mean to—"

" 'Only dolls,' " repeated the aunt, with icy significance. "Well, my child, you shall soon see what 'only' dolls can do."

"Won't she though!" cried Ganglia, and Vicky heard her stumble against the table, as though bent over with laughter.

"But what?" Vicky wailed, too terrified now to control herself. "What *are* you going to do? You keep talking about it, and hinting at it, but you never do anything! What *is* it?"

"We have already done it, my dear," said the aunt.

"Diadama!" cried the mother. "Be still! What are you thinking of?"

"Yeah," said Ganglia. "What we're going to do to her is for us to know and for her to find out."

"Yes . . . ," murmured the mother, creaking.

"And I think it *is* time for her to go to bed," said the aunt, sounding a bit flustered after her mistake. "She is forgetting herself."

Surprisingly enough, it was the living room they took her to, where the little velvet sofa was probably the softest place in the house. "And remember," said the mother as they left, "we don't sleep. We will be watching and waiting. Don't try anything rash."

"You must not leave this room," said the aunt. "And you will need the sleep for tomorrow."

"Yeah!" Ganglia squealed harshly, slammed the door, and they were gone.

But naturally Vicky couldn't sleep, and had no plans even to try. She huddled on the sofa, which, though padded, was scratchy and cold. She cried for awhile, feeling homesick for her own house, for the upright piano in the kitchen, for her father's cozy basement study, for her own room, all around her, but unattainable; and especially for the electric lights that kept the house bright at night. The thought of creeping by herself up the dark dollhouse stairs, with the dolls probably watching on every side, was almost too terrifying to imagine. Yet she could think of nothing else to do.

Then she remembered what they had said about falling into patterns. They didn't sleep, but perhaps they would be in their rooms, and the aunt hopefully under the kitchen table. It would have been better if the little door had not been right beside the bedrooms, but there was nothing she could do about that. And even if they caught her, she might at least discover something that would help her later. Steeling herself, Vicky sat up and took off her shoes.

Getting the door opened took quite a long time. She was afraid that it might squeak, or that one of them would be waiting in the hall, so she moved it very carefully, inch by inch. When it was opened just enough, she slipped quietly through.

She could barely see the stairs in the darkness, and behind her she felt the huge, empty silence of her bedroom. If she made one slip, they would be sure to hear. Feeling very small, she started cautiously up, remembering that the steps were steep, and keeping to the edge, where they would be less likely to creak. It was the bravest thing she had ever done in her life.

She stopped several times to listen, but all she could hear was the beating of her heart. She began moving more quickly as she neared the top of the steps. Perhaps she would get through the door after all!

There was only a short landing to cross at the top, but it was the most dangerous part, for the dolls were very close now. She heard the mother's dress rustle from the room beyond, and almost turned back. But the rustle did not come again; she had probably just been turning over in bed.

Tiptoeing now, Vicky moved across the landing, toward the door. In the darkness it was difficult to see, but as she neared it she made out a little knob, and could tell that the door was slightly ajar. It *was* real then, as she had hoped. She stopped beside it, holding her breath, and reached for the knob.

Something cold and fuzzy, like a snake with fur, wrapped itself around her wrist.

Vicky started to shriek, but she was so terrified, and the sensation was so horrible, that no sound came from her throat. She spun around, her skin crawling. Standing beside her, gripping her with his arm, was the father.

She caught her breath, and then, remembering her plan, put her finger to her lips. "Shhh!" she whispered. "Don't tell them, please don't. If you help me get out, I promise you, I promise I will do anything you want. They won't boss you around any more; they won't make you cry. I'll let you do it to them; I'll make you the king!" She peered into the darkness, trying to see his face. His arm was still tightly wrapped around her. "Anything!" she went on frantically. "Tell me what it is, and I'll do it. You'll be the ruler; they'll wait on you; they'll worship you; please, I'll—"

And then she heard a giggle behind her, and an indignant snort, and knew that she had failed.

"So *that's* what you'd do, is it?" came the mother's voice. "That sounds just marvelous for all the rest of us, I must say. After hearing that, do you think we'd even consider letting you get away?"

"She sounded so stupid, whispering like that," Ganglia snickered.

"But," said Vicky, beginning to cry, "but I didn't mean it. I promise I won't—"

"We've had enough of your promises!" snapped the mother.

"This is our reward for giving her a comfortable place to sleep," said the aunt.

"Yes," said the mother. "You see I was right, Quimbee, to make you wait there for her."

The father cleared his throat. "Of course, of course, I never would have considered her offer."

"I'll bet you wouldn't have," Ganglia sneered. "It's a good thing you knew we were watching you."

"And she's certainly not getting a comfortable bed after that," said the mother. "She'll spend the night up here, next to us, in the playroom, on the floor. Dandaroo, you stay with her and don't let her make a move. I'm going back to bed. These odious patterns we're stuck with! But they'll go away after we've had her here for a month or two."

Vicky hardly noticed being pushed into the playroom, hardly noticed their last angry remarks or their retreating footsteps. She sank to the floor, weeping bitterly, for now there was no hope at all. Both of her plans had failed miserably.

"Hey," said a small, reedy voice and something touched her shoulder. "Hey, stop crying, please."

She sat up, her shoulders still jerking.

"Please," Dandaroo went on, very quietly. She glanced behind him and saw that he had shut the door. "Please, stop crying. I'll try to help you. I'll try to get you through the attic door."

"You will?" she gasped.

"I hate them!" he said fiercely. "I hate the way they always push me around. If you'll promise to—"

"Yes, yes, I'll do anything, I'll do anything," she said, her voice rising with excitement. "If only you'll get me out, I'll do anything you want, anything!"

"Shhh! If the others hear we won't have a chance."

"But will you really get me out? Really?" Then she stopped suddenly. "Oh, but how can you?" she moaned, thinking of how helpless and weak he was. "What could you do?"

Dandaroo sighed and looked toward the door, then sat down heavily beside her. "I'll help you get up to the attic. That's the best I can do. After that, it will all be up to you."

"But why the attic?" she asked, leaning toward him. "I didn't even know there *was* an attic before. Why will it make any difference if I go up there?"

"Because," Dandaroo said, and then he paused and looked away for a moment, as if he were suddenly afraid to answer her.

"Why?" Vicky insisted.

"Because . . . because that's where the dollhouse is," he said in a hushed voice.

"The *dollhouse*?" For a moment Vicky was too confused to know what to say. "You mean there's another dollhouse inside this one?"

He nodded.

"But why? What kind of dollhouse is it?"

"It's not like this house, with old-fashioned furniture and stuff inside. It's more modern, and it has lights, and plumbing, and a bathroom, and everything. And it has a living room, and a kitchen with a piano in it—"

Vicky started, then peered at him intently.

"—and a dining room, and two bedrooms, and a study in the basement for the father." He paused.

"And it has three dolls," he went on slowly. "A mother, a father, and—"

"And a little girl?" said Vicky breathlessly.

"Yes," said Dandaroo, watching her face. "A little girl. Only the little girl isn't there any more."

Chapter Seven

In the distance there was a vast, invisible sigh as the curtains in Vicky's bedroom moved in a midnight breeze. But she did not notice, still trying to make out Dandaroo's dim features. Her mind was whirling with confusion; and a kind of dizzying excitement, touched with hope, was rising inside her.

"The dollhouse in the attic," she said, twisting her hands. "It's my house, isn't it?"

Dandaroo nodded.

"And the dolls in it. They're my mother, and father, and . . . and me?"

"Only you aren't in it any more." Again, he looked apprehensively toward the door.

"But wait a minute." She brought her voice down to a whisper again. "Tell me something first. Do you . . . do you and the other dolls *play* with that dollhouse, do you play with the dolls in it?"

Dandaroo laughed; a short, mirthless grunt. "If you can call it that. They do things to them, yes indeed. Every time we get a minute to ourselves, up we go to the attic. Up we go, to tip the mother down the stairs, to make her yell at the father and punish the little girl. Ganglia and the mother, they enjoy it the most, of course."

Without seeing, Vicky stared off into her bedroom. "So that's why . . . why everything's been so strange recently. The dolls are doing it."

"Yes. Because you were doing it to them."

Vicky turned on him. "That isn't fair! It's not the same. I thought you were just dolls, that it didn't matter, that you couldn't feel anything. But you *knew* we were real."

"That didn't make any difference. They just wanted to get back at you."

Vicky was puzzling it out. Perhaps she felt a little guilty, but another thought was uppermost in her mind: If she could ever get out of here, she could get that little dollhouse away from them, and then the terrible things would stop happening in her family. If she could get out.

"The little girl doll. What did you mean when you said she wasn't there any more?"

"Ganglia took her out of the dollhouse. That's why you're here."

"But why did she? And where is the doll? Tell me everything; you've got to!"

"Shhh! Keep your voice down. They'll kill us if they find out. They could be listening, you know."

"All right, all right. Just tell me."

Dandaroo sighed. "It was the mother's idea. She started wondering what would happen if we took you out. It might mean that you would get lost away from home, or something else unpleasant, or even that you would be caught in here. It was at lunch today. And when you made her send Ganglia up to her room, that was the perfect opportunity to find out. So when you weren't looking, Ganglia sneaked up to the attic, and took the little girl doll out of the house." He paused.

"Go on! Go on!"

"Well, three of us were sitting at the table, and your great big face was right beside the room, breathing on us; and then suddenly it was gone. And Ganglia came tearing down the stairs, screaming that she'd taken out the doll. Taken it out, and then lost it."

"*Lost* it?" said Vicky, a cold wave of horror running through her. "She lost it?"

"She said she'd taken out the doll, and then it suddenly was gone. She must have dropped it. But she looked everywhere for it, she said, everywhere, and couldn't find it. So of course the mother was furious. She thought Ganglia had ruined everything, and sent her right back up to her room. And then, we noticed that the music box was on, and the aunt went to see what was happening. And there you were."

"Lost it?" Vicky repeated bleakly. "Didn't anyone else try to find it?"

"Oh yes. That's why they sent the father and me up to the attic. We looked everywhere, but we couldn't find it."

"And I . . . I suppose," said Vicky, trying to hold back the tears that, once again, were threatening to overcome her, "I suppose if you could find the doll, and put it back in the dollhouse, then I'd be back in my own house again?"

"Yes," said Dandaroo solemnly. "That's the only way."

"How could she lose it? How could she *lose* it?" Vicky moaned, clenching her fists.

"I don't know how. It's just like her, though. But one thing is, it's got to be up in the attic, somewhere. Your only chance is to go up there, and find it, and put it back in the house. And I'll help you get up there."

She was studying his face again, suspiciously. "But why? Why are you on my side?"

He looked down at the floor. "You know I'm not

like the others. I haven't been here as long. And I hate them! They're always picking on me. If you got out, you could make them stop." Suddenly she felt her hand in his blunt, desperate grip. "But if I help you get out, you've got to remember me, please, remember to make me safe, the minute you get out, or else . . ." He let her hand drop. "Or else, you know the kind of things they would do. And the other reason I'm helping you is . . . you never played with me much, I guess. You never made me do anything mean. So I'm not cruel like they are. I don't want to see them make you their slave."

"Their *slave*?"

"Shhh! Yes, their slave. That's what they want to do with you. They've already thought up all kinds of chores for you, like bringing all the furniture up and down the stairs to different rooms, and polishing the walls and the ceilings and the roof, and waiting on them. . . . But it isn't right. You're different from us; you're not a doll; you don't belong in here. That's why . . . why I'll help you."

This time, her tears were not for herself. She reached out and touched his rough sleeve. "Thanks," she said. There was a long silence, while he continued to stare, embarrassed, at the floor. "Thanks," she said again, softly. "I won't forget. I promise I won't."

He cleared his throat. "Yes. If you get out. But it won't be easy." He looked at her. "They'll be listening every instant, of course. If they hear so much as a creak or a footstep out there, they'll be at you again. The only thing to do is get them away from that door. What I can do is pretend you ran downstairs. I'll start yelling that you ran away, downstairs, and make a lot of noise, and hopefully they'll all run down there after me, without thinking. The aunt is down there already. And that's your chance. You've got to hurry up to the attic and *find that doll*. Once you've got it, you're safe. Just put it back in the dollhouse. But you won't have much time. They'll catch on quick enough and be back up there, looking for you. And if they catch you, and you haven't found the doll, then . . . then I don't want to think about what will happen next. And it will be just as bad for me."

"You mean I have to go up there *alone*?"

"But how else can we do it?" he said with exasperation. "I'm doing everything I can."

"Okay. I'm sorry." She looked away for a moment, thinking. Then she pushed her hair back and stood up. She took a deep breath. "Okay," she said. "I'm ready, I guess. Let's get going."

She never would have thought that Dandaroo,

who was always so quiet, could make so much noise. His solid, stiff little body was suddenly a darting whirlwind of energy as he sped, thumping and shrieking, out of the room. "She's running away, she's running away!" he screamed, already clattering down the stairs. "She's going downstairs, she's getting away. Downstairs! Downstairs! She's getting awaaaaay!"

The noise and confusion on the landing were instantaneous. "You fool! You simpleton!" came the harsh voices of Ganglia and the mother, and "Dear! Dear!" she heard the father mutter, as momentarily their footsteps and rustlings filled the hallway. And Dandaroo had been right. They were in a fury to catch her, and no one waited to guard the stairway to the attic. Before she knew it, they were down the steps. It was time now, and she didn't have a second to lose.

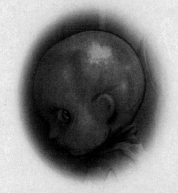

Chapter Eight

The doorway was very low, and it did creak, but that didn't matter now. She was through it in a moment and on the steps. They were even steeper than the others, and very narrow. In the darkness she could barely see, and kept bumping against the wall as she stumbled up.

Something thick and sticky brushed against her face at the top. A spiderweb. She saw now that the attic was full of them. They were not doll size, of course, but real; and they were draped, in the gray dimness, across whole walls, hanging loosely from the pitched roof to the floor, all stirring slightly. Vicky did not allow herself the time to wonder very long about their inhabitants, but she was shivering as she peered around the room.

The attic was the one place in the house that was completely enclosed, and Vicky would not have been able to see at all if it had not been for the small round window in front. The first pale beginnings of daylight were beginning to filter through it, falling coldly on the few dusty pieces of junk: a bit of black ribbon in the corner; a hatpin, like a sword, leaning against the wall; a dried-up wad of chewing gum, the size of her head. But her eyes stopped at once on one very strange and beautiful thing. Transfixed, she moved slowly toward it.

The house was large, and sat proudly on an old spool in the center of the room. Every detail was absolutely perfect; but for the one missing wall, it resembled her house in every way. She was fascinated by the little light bulbs, the miniature faucet, and the tiny droplets, like silvery motes of dust, dripping into the sink; the perfect little piano, on which her thumb alone would play an octave; the magazines and books, the newspapers covered with a gray blur; the intricacy of the stairways; the rugs and the furniture.

But most perfect of all were the dolls. Her father was curled up uncomfortably on the couch in his study, his face a delicate pink, his little fingers almost too small to see, each thin strand of his hair fashioned separately. Her mother lay on her stomach in the bedroom, the tiny bones in her shoulders as fragile as match sticks, her waist the size of Vicky's finger. They looked so real, but were they? Vicky wondered. Were they breathing, or were they just perfect little dolls?

It was very strange to be looking down at this tiny replica of her house and family; and all the more disconcerting because until a moment ago she had felt very tiny, but now she felt like a giant. Which was she? She could not decide.

But she had no time to wonder now. Downstairs she could hear distant footsteps and squeals. Had they caught on yet? She had to find that doll! For an instant, the thought of the fragile little thing lost in this unruly household made her heart stand still. What if it should get broken, what would happen to her? Stop it! she ordered herself. Stop thinking and look!

On her knees, she ran her hands rapidly over the floor around and underneath the house, toward the stairs; perhaps Ganglia had dropped it as she ran. There was nothing but dust. She moved toward the ribbon, pawing at the floor, ignoring the spiderwebs clinging to her face and her hair. There was nothing but dust. Behind the hatpin she searched, behind the wad of gum, each place more and more unlikely. Into the dark corners where the ceiling met the floor, into the thickest webs, her face grimy, her skirt torn. And there was nothing, nothing but dust.

And now she heard the dolls on the stairs, their voices growing closer. If only she hadn't spent so much time staring at the house! She jumped to her feet, coughing and gasping, and began running her hands frantically over the lowest beams and rafters. Her fingers closed around something soft—and then she dropped, with a shudder of disgust, the remains of a fly as large as her forearm. It was no good. The little doll was nowhere.

The dolls were on the attic stairs. Not knowing what else to do, she backed toward the house, spreading her arms protectively behind her.

Ganglia burst into the room, stopping suddenly at the top of the stairs. The aunt rose up stiffly behind her, and the father; and then the mother elbowed her way through them, pushing Dandaroo ahead of her, her arm wrapped tightly around his neck. Now there was no doubt at all that his face could have expressions, for in his eyes there was agony and despair.

"So," said the mother quite softly, her head wobbling, while the others waited, suddenly silent. Though her voice trembled with fury, her face, as always, was bland and cherubic. "So, you've disobeyed us again, and you've found our toy, with the help of this sniveling little monster." She squeezed

Dandaroo's neck, and he squirmed. "But little good it's going to do you; very little good. You'll never get away now, you've missed your chance. Ganglia, get the hatpin!" she said sharply, then turned back to Vicky. "And now," she went on, even more softly, after a pause. "And now, before we do anything to you, you will have the pleasure of watching us 'play' with the two dolls that are left."

Vicky took a step backward, blocking the house with her body. Though filled with terror, her mind was very clear. "Where did you lose it, Ganglia?" she said, her voice shaking. "Where is it? Just tell me where you lost the doll. I can do anything you want, you know I can!"

"But I tell you, I didn't *lose* it!" Ganglia cried, stamping her foot and almost dropping the hatpin. "Everybody thinks I lost it, but I didn't." She turned to the mother. "It just disappeared. As soon as I took it out of the house, it vanished into thin air, right in my hand. Why doesn't anybody believe me?"

Vanished into thin air. Vicky's mind was racing now, as the mother and the other dolls began moving purposefully toward her, Ganglia awkwardly brandishing the hatpin, which looked very sharp. *Into thin air.* Those little dolls were so realistic. . . . For an instant she looked down at herself. And then the thought came to her: Perhaps *she* was the doll.

Perhaps, when Ganglia had taken it out of the dolls' dollhouse, her little doll self and her real self outside had somehow come together into one being, had merged in the in-between world of her dollhouse. The doll had vanished, there had to be a reason for it; she had vanished from her bedroom, and here she was. It must be the answer. She and the doll were the same thing.

The dolls were close now, surrounding her and the house in a half circle; silent, but for Dandaroo's gasps, their expressionless faces were looming over her. She stepped backward again, until her dress was actually touching the house.

And if it were true, that she and the doll of herself were now the same thing, then the way to get back would be to go into the dollhouse herself. She spun around. But how, how? The dollhouse was so small, she could never fit inside.

And then the aunt's arm was on her neck, and she felt the point of the hatpin pierce her dress and press coldly into her back. There was nothing to do but try. It was her last hope. Just as the aunt began to pull her away, she stuck her hand into the little bedroom.

It was like the force she had felt before, but in reverse. She was being pulled into the house, too strongly to resist. The aunt's hand slipped away behind; she felt rushing movement all around her and the odd sensation of shrinking and growing at the same time, of being sucked into a kind of whirlwind. And, fading away into the distance, Dandaroo's wailing cry, "Remember meeeeee!"

And then she was lying on her own bedroom floor, in the pale dawn light from her own windows. She rose to her feet, a bit bewildered, but filled nevertheless with soaring joy and relief. "I'm home," she said softly, "I'm home again," and then she shouted from sheer happiness and leaped into the air.

In the next moment, her cry caught in her throat and she turned to the dollhouse. They were all still in there, up in the attic, and at any instant they could simply take her out of their dollhouse again, and there she would be, just as trapped as before. She had to get that dollhouse out of there, before they had a chance to take her out of it and bring her back to them.

Chapter Nine

Vicky fell to her knees and began tugging at the wall just below the roof, the wall that covered the attic. It seemed to be nailed tightly in place and would not move. Dandaroo must be keeping them away from the dollhouse; if not, they would have taken her out instantly. "Keep fighting, Dandaroo, keep them away!" she shouted, pulling at the wood, shaking the whole house. The dishes rattled and the living room lamp tipped over, but the wall stayed in place.

Should she run down and get her father's hammer and pry it off? But that would take too long; they'd have her before she even got back. "Keep fighting, Dandaroo," she moaned, her voice choked with fear; and then her hand brushed accidentally against a little knob at the side of the house, and the attic wall sprang open.

It had only been just in time. Ganglia, the father,

and the aunt all had their arms wrapped around Dandaroo, standing just to the side of the tiny house. In front of it stood the mother, reaching toward it. Her hand shaking, Vicky pushed the mother away; the doll fell stiffly, helplessly to the floor. Carefully, very carefully, she picked up the dolls' dollhouse. She was going to have to find a safe place for it, a very safe place, she decided as she lifted it out. But the moment it was out of the dollhouse the little building simply faded away.

For a moment Vicky stared, amazed, at her empty hand. But of course, she realized, it would have to happen that way. Just as she and the doll had become one in the dollhouse, so now, in the real world, the dolls' dollhouse would become one with her house, and the dolls' little dolls would merge with her and her parents.

But she still had something very important to do. Carefully she pulled the dolls' arms away from Dandaroo, leaving them lying carelessly on the dusty floor, and very gently she lifted him out. "A safe place," she said softly. "I'll find you a good safe place, and they'll never hurt you again."

She left him at last on her pillow, and then went to clean herself before going down to breakfast. It was then she noticed that she was not wearing shoes. She hurried back to the dollhouse, and there they were, smaller than her little finger, beside the living room couch. She wondered how she would explain their loss to her mother and father. She did not know quite what to expect from her parents or what their attitude would be toward her absence.

To her relief, they did not seem to have noticed that she had been gone at all. And much more important, they had gone back to being their old selves: The influence of the dolls must have vanished along with their dollhouse. It would have seemed that nothing could make Vicky happier than she already was, until her mother, studying her face, said, "You look tired, dear. You've been so droopy recently." She turned to her father, "You know, I think it's that dollhouse."

"Yes," her father agreed, laying down his knife and fork. "She's been spending altogether too much time with that thing. She should be outdoors more. Would you mind terribly, Vicky, if we got rid of it?"

"Get rid of it?" Vicky said, hardly able to believe what he was saying. "Get rid of it? No, no, I wouldn't mind at all."

It was not long after that that she came home from school to find her room cleansed of its presence. Dandaroo had not gone with it; she had hidden him in a cotton-padded box in her drawer.

"Where did you throw the dollhouse away?" she said to her mother.

"Throw it away?" her mother said. "A valuable thing like that? Don't be ridiculous, darling. We sold it to the Larners. They told me that Judy was longing for a dollhouse. I'm sure it will be a treasure to her."

"But," Vicky started to warn her. "But you shouldn't have—" Then she stopped. Perhaps, if another girl played differently with the dolls, then they would change. There was no way of knowing. But it did seem that it was beyond her control; whatever would happen with the dollhouse now was not for her to decide. But she kept Dandaroo to herself for the rest of her life.

Among the Dolls

WILLIAM SLEATOR

ABOUT THIS GUIDE

The information, activities, and discussion questions which follow
are intended to enhance your reading of *Among the Dolls*. Please
feel free to adapt these materials to suit your needs and interests.

ABOUT THE AUTHOR

William Sleator, the eldest child of a pediatrician mother and a
scientist father, grew up in St. Louis, Missouri. He began writing
stories and composing music at the age of six. In 1967, he received bachelor's degrees in music and English from Harvard
University. He next studied musical composition and worked as a
pianist at the Royal Ballet School in England. An avid journal
keeper, Sleator recorded his experiences living in an ancient English cottage which he brought to life in his first young adult novel,
Blackbriar. After nine years working as a rehearsal pianist for the
Boston Ballet—and composing music for three ballets—Sleator
turned to writing full-time. Many of his award-winning books and
stories imagine strange applications of real scientific phenomena,
while another recurring motif is the impact of architectural sur-
roundings, such as the many variants of the Tithonus home in *The
Green Futures of Tycho* or Vicky's adventures inside the mysteri-
ous dollhouse in *Among the Dolls*.

Sleator divides his time between Bangkok, Thailand, and Boston, Massachusetts. On his website biography, he comments about his profession: "I consider myself extremely fortunate to be able to make a living as a writer. I shouldn't ever run out of ideas—knock on wood—since the universe is full of great things like strange attractors and the Mandelbrot set. I still can't get over the fact that time slows down in the presence of a gravitational field. It really does, you know. That's not science fiction. It's a fact."

WRITING AND RESEARCH ACTIVITIES
I. A QUESTION OF SIZE

A. From *Gulliver's Travels* to *Alice's Adventures in Wonderland*, the notion of experiencing life from a different size perspective has fascinated fantasy writers. Go to the library or online to make a list of books in which characters change size or encounter characters sized differently than themselves. Using a computer to incorporate graphics and use varied fonts, make an illustrated "Incredible Shrinking Reading List."

B. Keep a "Size Journal" in which to record observations and thoughts after the following activities:

1. Spend an hour watching a toddler or preschooler, noting how he or she navigates steps, reaches items on countertops, climbs into an adult-sized chair, and so on.

2. Recall a time when you were told you had to "wait until you are bigger" to get a certain toy or participate in an activity. Write about this memory and your current thoughts and feelings looking back on the event.

3. Make a list of interesting words that describe the size of things. If desired, use a dictionary or thesaurus and include interesting phrases on your list.

4. Describe the activities of an ant or other small insect, the way a big dog and a little dog play together, or another animal activity related to size.

C. Write a short story in which you, or a character similar to yourself, are transformed in size. Describe the transformation. How do you feel? What happens to you in your new size? What does the world look like? What are the advantages and disadvantages of living life this size? Can you control this change? What do you learn from this experience?

II. TOYS ALIVE!

A. Have you ever wished a favorite doll, toy, or game could come to life? With classmates or friends, write and enact a scene in which you enter your bedroom or playroom to discover one or more toys come to life. What is your reaction? What does the toy have to say to you? What do you do together? What else happens?

B. Select and watch a video in which a toy comes to life, such as *Toy Story* or *Pinocchio*. Then, imagine you are the host of a television program that reviews and discusses films. On your own, or with friends or classmates, present your review of the movie, including your thoughts on why people are intrigued by the toy-come-to-life theme.

C. Choose your favorite chapter or short excerpt from *Among the Dolls* to develop into a movie. Create a storyboard (a series of cartoon-style drawings depicting the scene) or a 1–2 page description outlining how you would transform this chapter into a movie scene.

III. REAL AND PRETEND

A. The line between real life and pretend (or imagined or toy) life is intriguingly blurred in *Among the Dolls*. Divide a sheet of paper into two columns headed with the terms "real" and "pretend." Beneath each term, write your own definition, followed by a dictionary definition. Then, list key real and pretend experiences Vicky has in the novel in the appropriate columns. Are there moments, thoughts, or experiences which seem to hover between the real and the pretend column? List these on the back of the page.

B. Have you ever awakened from a dream certain it had really happened? Have you ever looked into the eyes of a pet or doll and felt like you saw an expression of true understanding? Write a short essay describing a life experience of your own which seemed to have elements of both the real and the pretend.

C. The way Vicky treats the dollhouse dolls can be seen as a reflection of her real-life emotions and attitudes. With classmates or friends, discuss how the ways people treat their clothes, toys, homes, and classrooms sheds light on other aspects of their character.

D. Think about your own behavior toward objects. Do you put your clothes away neatly, clean your room, and respect school property? How would you describe the way you play with games and sports equipment? What do you do if a toy gets broken? Have you ever damaged an object because you felt angry at a person? Write a paragraph, a poem, or lyrics to a song in which you answer one or more of these questions and explore how you feel about what you have realized.

E. William Sleator, a journal keeper, member of a large family, and talented musician, incorporates many aspects of his own, real life into his works of fantasy and science fiction. Go online to learn more about the writer before composing a brief essay entitled, "Where Real Meets Pretend in the Stories of William Sleator."

DISCUSSION QUESTIONS

1. Where do Vicky and her parents drive in the first chapter of *Among the Dolls*? What strange person does Vicky see there?

2. What birthday gift does Vicky dream of receiving? What does she receive instead? What might her conclusion that it ". . . was undoubtedly the worst birthday she had ever had" tell readers about Vicky?

3. Had you been Vicky, would you have responded to the doll-house in the same way? Why or why not? Have you ever been disappointed by receiving—or not receiving—a particular gift? How did you react?

4. What bothers Vicky about the dollhouse? How does she propose to fix this problem? How does her mother feel about Vicky's solution?

5. As Vicky begins to take an interest in the dollhouse, how does her schoolwork and home life begin to change?

6. What events lead Vicky into the dollhouse? Are the events themselves important? Why or why not?

7. How do the furniture, foods, toys, and dolls seem different to Vicky when she perceives them from inside the dollhouse?

8. What is unusual about the dolls' names? How did they get these names?

9. How do the dolls feel about Vicky? How do the dolls behave toward each other? What are the dolls' plans for doll-sized Vicky?

10. At the end of Chapter Two, what does the aunt doll mean when she tells Vicky, "It is you, after all, who has made us what we are?" Does the aunt doll recall another character in the story?

11. In the dollhouse, Vicky is called "small and helpless." Is this different from the way she seems to feel about herself in her human-sized life?

12. What plans does Vicky consider for escaping from the doll-house? Who ultimately helps Vicky to reach the secret door? How is Dandaroo different from the other dolls?

13. How does the author describe the dollhouse attic? What does Vicky discover there? What happens when the dolls find her in the attic?

14. How does Vicky escape from the little dollhouse? What becomes of the toy dollhouse in the attic?

15. How is Vicky's home life different when she returns from her dollhouse experience? What do her parents decide to do with the dollhouse?

16. Does Vicky do anything to try to protect the toy's new owner? Why or why not?

17. Do you think Vicky has been changed by her experience among the dolls? What does she do with Dandaroo? Why do you think she does this?

18. Have you ever wondered if a doll or toy could come to life? Have you ever wanted to be rid of a toy? Have you ever played roughly with a toy as a reaction to some real-life experience? Describe your thoughts in these situations.

19. Do you think a game of pretend, or an experience playing with a toy can affect your real life or the way you think about things? Why or why not?

20. What do you think happened when Ganglia took the little girl doll from the attic house? What does Vicky come to believe about the missing doll? Do you think Vicky's adventure in the dollhouse was a real event, a dream, or another sort of experience? Explain your answer.